THE FRIENDLY
PIRATES

SAVIOUR PIROTTA
ILLUSTRATED BY **ERICA SALCEDO**

D0493377

BLOOMSBURY EDUCATION
Bloomsbury Publishing Plc
50 Bedford Square, London, WC1B 3DP, UK

BLOOMSBURY, BLOOMSBURY EDUCATION and the Diana logo
are trademarks of Bloomsbury Publishing Plc

First published in Great Britain 2019 by Bloomsbury Publishing Plc
Text copyright © Saviour Pirotta, 2019
Illustrations copyright © Erica Salcedo, 2019

Saviour Pirotta and Erica Salcedo have asserted their rights under the Copyright, Designs
and Patents Act, 1988, to be identified as Author and Illustrator of this work

This is a work of fiction. Names and characters are the product of the author's imagination
and any resemblance to actual persons, living or dead, is entirely coincidental.

A catalogue record for this book is available from the British Library

ISBN: PB: 978-1-4729-5980-5; ePDF: 978-1-4729-5979-9; ePub: 978-1-4729-5981-2;
enhanced ePub: 978-1-4729-6952-1

2 4 6 8 10 9 7 5 3 1

P[...], Guangdong

All [...] [...]clable products
from [...] rocesses conform [...]igin.

[...] [...]ore about our [...] [...]books that w w w.[...]msbury.com

Chapter One

Adam, Amy and Ali were pirates. They
lived on Cutlass Island.

It was lovely there. The sun shone nearly
every day. The sea was warm and clear
as glass. Millions of stars twinkled in
the night sky.

"There's only one problem with this place," said Amy one evening. "It's just too quiet." "I wish we could go and live in the big city," sighed Adam. "It would be so exciting."

Sadly, Cutlass Island was thousands of miles away from the big city. And the pirates had no ship. It had sunk.

Far away in the big city lived three glamorous ballet dancers. Their names were Melanie, Mario and Marta. Every night they danced in their glittery costumes. The audience cheered wildly. Sometimes people sent them expensive gifts.

"There's only one problem with the big city," sighed Marta one night. "It's far too busy. Oh, for a bit of peace and quiet."
Melanie looked thoughtful. "Listen up. I have an idea..."

A few weeks later, Ali woke up in the
middle of the night to see a ship in the bay.
"Wake up, me hearties," he said,
prodding Amy and Adam.
Amy peered through her telescope.
"A ship! Now's our chance to get
away from Cutlass Island."

The pirates swam out to the ship and clambered on board.

They hid in a chest near the mast.

Chapter Two

Early next morning, the pirates heard feet stomping across the deck.

"That's enough fruit and water to last us," said a voice.

"Back to the high seas," said another.

"This is far better than life in the ballet," laughed a third.

It was the dancers. They had bought a ship and run away to sea. The chest the pirates had hidden in was really a costume hamper.

For most of the day, life on the ship was pretty quiet. Then...

"What's that?" cried Marta. A giant
wiggly tentacle was looming up over
the deck. More followed, until six slimy
tentacles had surrounded the ship. Last
of all came a big round head with fierce
eyes and lots of sharp teeth.

"It's a sea monster," screamed Mario as the ship trembled.

"To arms," called Melanie. The dancers had brought swords with them. They'd learned stage fighting at ballet school. But there were only three of them and the monster had six tentacles.

"I'm afraid we're all doomed unless we help them," whispered Ali, peeping out of the costume hamper. "We'll have to reveal ourselves."

With a great whoop, the pirates leapt out. Six swords flashed in the evening sun.

The monster fought back but it soon realised it couldn't win and slid back under the waves.

"I have no idea where you lot came from," said Melanie to the pirates. "But thank you for your help."

Chapter Three

The ballet dancers stopped at the next port to repair their damaged ship. The pirates went ashore and Melanie gave them a purse full of gold, so they could stay at a comfortable inn.

The city was as exciting as the pirates had imagined. There were cake shops and ice-cream parlours and parks with fairgrounds that never shut.

"The only problem with this place,"
sighed Adam, a month after they'd
arrived in the city, "is that it's too noisy,
even after bedtime. I can't sleep."
"And it's very expensive," said Ali.
"We're nearly out of gold."

"I miss the stars," said Amy. "I wish we could go back to Cutlass Island."
"We might have just enough gold left to buy a little sailing boat," said Ali.

The pirates went down to the harbour, where they soon discovered they didn't even have enough money for a canoe, let alone a sailing boat. But they found a battered old boat abandoned on the shore. They could see the name painted on it in fading letters: the *Rub-A-Tub-Tub*.

For the next few weeks, the pirates worked at repairing the boat. Ali spent their very last penny on an old bed sheet, which they patched and darned to make a sail.

Chapter Four

They finally set off home. When they
were out in the middle of the ocean,
Ali heard someone shouting.
"Help! Help!"
A man stood on the shore of a tiny
island, waving.
The pirates steered towards him.

"Glad to see you," said the man.
"Captain Rawley's the name. My
sailors turned on me and left me here.
Will you take me with you?"
"We're on our way home," said Ali.
"We'll drop you off at the nearest
port, if you like."

As they sailed away from the island, Captain Rawley was all smiles. But once they were back on the open sea, he suddenly pulled out a dagger.

"Put your hands up," he snarled. Before the pirates knew it, he'd pushed them down into the hold and locked the trapdoor.

"I usually feed my prisoners to the sharks," he laughed. "But since you've been nice enough to let me have your boat, I shall drop you in the sea when we sight land. Then you can swim ashore."

"He's really a pirate, isn't he?" Adam shuddered. "A really bad pirate!"

Chapter Five

The hours passed and the moon came up. Ali was the only one of the pirates still awake. Suddenly he heard a thud on the deck, followed by the clash of swords.

The trapdoor was lifted and Mario peered down into the hold.

"Wake up," he said. "We spotted your ship through the telescope and saw that horrible man lock you up. Good job we happened to be passing by."

The ballet dancers had tied Captain Rawley to the mast and taken away his dagger.

"Let me go," he begged, "I'll give you my treasure map..."

Melanie found the map in his jacket pocket.

"It's a deal," she said. "You can have the lifeboat from our ship. But you have to stop being a bad pirate. You could be a good one, like our friends."

With Captain Rawley gone, the pirates thanked the ballet dancers for saving them.

"The High Seas are a bit too quiet
for city folk like us," explained Mario.
"We're going home."
"And the city is too noisy for pirates like us,"
said Ali. "We're on our way home too."

So the dancers went home and joined the ballet company again. And the pirates settled back into their quiet life on Cutlass Island. Only, once a year, they sailed to the city and joined the ballet dancers on stage for the Christmas pantomime.

And when the theatre shut for the summer, the three ballet dancers raised the sails and went treasure hunting with the pirates.